It's the Great Pumpkin, Charlie Brown™

By Charles M. Schulz

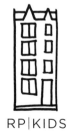

RP | KIDS

PHILADELPHIA · LONDON

© 2010 by United Feature Syndicate, Inc.

All rights reserved under the Pan-American and International Copyright Conventions

Printed in China

PEANUTS © United Feature Syndicate, Inc. PEANUTS is a registered trademark of United Feature Syndicate, Inc. All rights reserved.

This book may not be reproduced in whole or in part, in any form or by any means, electronic or mechanical, including photocopying, recording, or by any information storage and retrieval system now known or hereafter invented, without written permission from the publisher.

9
Digit on the right indicates the number of this printing

Library of Congress Control Number: 2009926790
ISBN 978-0-7624-3826-6

Text adapted by Lauryn Tuchman
Art Adapted by Tom Brannon
Cover and interior design by Frances J. Soo Ping Chow
Typography: Abadi, Bembo, and Chuck 2

Published by Running Press Kids
An Imprint of Running Press Book Publishers
A Member of the Perseus Books Group
2300 Chestnut Street
Philadelphia, PA 19103-4371

Visit us on the web!
www.runningpress.com/rpkids
www.snoopy.com

IT WAS A BRISK AUTUMN DAY.

But it wasn't just any autumn day—it was Halloween.
Charlie Brown was busy raking leaves while Snoopy
was busy playing in them.

Lucy stopped by with a football.

"How about practicing some plays, Charlie Brown?" asked Lucy. "I'll hold the ball, and you come running and kick it."

"You must think I'm really stupid," replied Charlie Brown. "You just want me to come running up to the ball so you can pull it away and watch me fall flat on my back."

"This time you can trust me," said Lucy, flashing a toothy grin.

But Charlie Brown didn't believe her.

"No," answered Charlie Brown. "No, no, and no!"

"Please, Charlie Brown," pleaded Lucy. "I have a signed document testifying that I will not pull the ball away."

Charlie Brown grabbed the piece of paper and studied it. "It *is* signed. I guess if you have a signed document in your hand you can't go wrong. It looks like I'm really going to kick the football this year."

With that, Charlie Brown backed up...and charged.

Just as he was about to kick the ball, Lucy pulled it away,

and Charlie Brown fell flat on his back!

"ARGH!" Charlie Brown screamed in pain.

Lucy picked up the piece of paper. "Funny thing—

this signed document was never notarized."

Meanwhile, Linus was inside writing an important letter.

Dear Great Pumpkin. I'm looking forward to your arrival on Halloween night.

Charlie Brown approached his friend. "What are you writing, Linus?"

"It's the time of year to write a letter to the Great Pumpkin," answered Linus.

"Who?" asked Charlie Brown, looking confused.

"Every year on Halloween night the Great Pumpkin rises up out of his pumpkin patch and flies through the air with bags of toys for children everywhere," explained Linus.

After Charlie Brown left, Linus continued writing his letter.

You must get discouraged because more people believe in Santa Claus than in you. Santa does get more publicity and that might make you number two, but that means that you really just need to try harder.

Just then, Lucy and Peppermint Patty appeared.

"Oh, brother," moaned Lucy. "Linus, are you writing a letter to that stupid pumpkin *again*?"

Linus nodded.

"I am the laughing stock of the neighborhood because every year my little brother writes a letter to the Great Pumpkin!" cried Lucy and stormed off.

Sally appeared just as Linus was signing his letter.

"What are you doing, Linus?" asked Sally.

Linus hesitated and then answered, "I'm writing to the Great Pumpkin. He rises out of the pumpkin patch on Halloween night and brings bags of toys for children everywhere."

"Oh, Linus," swooned Sally. "You say the cutest things."

"Hey, Sally, would you like to sit with me in the pumpkin patch on Halloween night and wait for the Great Pumpkin together?" asked Linus.

Sally's eyes lit up. "Oh, Linus. I'd love to!"

Linus went to mail his letter.

"Really, Linus," cried Lucy. "Just *how* do you think you are going to mail that letter anyway? You can't possibly reach the mailbox, and I'm not going to help you."

Linus whipped his blanket in the air, hooked a corner of it onto the handle, and pulled open the mailbox. He then sent his letter flying in the air. Lucy watched as the letter slid into the opened mailbox.

"Like that," replied a triumphant Linus, and he walked away.

Just then, Charlie Brown ran up waving a piece of paper in his hand.

"Hey!" exclaimed Charlie Brown. "I got an invitation to Violet's Halloween party!"

Lucy rolled her eyes. "Oh, brother," she said with a sneer, "Charlie Brown, if you got an invitation then it must have been a mistake."

"Lucy, do you know if Linus is going to the party?" asked Sally.

Lucy sighed. "Probably not. That blockhead brother of mine will be out in the pumpkin patch making a fool of himself just like he does every year."

"But maybe there really is a Great Pumpkin," said Sally.

"Do I get to go trick-or-treating this year?" Sally asked her big brother.

"Sure, Sally," replied Charlie Brown.

"Oh boy . . . oh boy!" exclaimed Sally. "How do we do it?"

"It's very simple," Lucy said. "All you have to do is walk up to a house and ring the doorbell. When the person opens the door, say 'tricks or treats!'"

Sally looked suspicious. "Are you sure that's legal?"

"Oh, good grief!" Lucy cringed. "Of course it's legal!"

Everyone met later that afternoon at Lucy's house in their costumes.

"A person should always pick a costume which is in direct contrast to one's own personality," said Lucy as she lowered a witch mask over her face.

Lucy looked Charlie Brown up and down. "Really, Charlie Brown, what are you supposed to be anyway?"

Charlie Brown responded from underneath the cut up sheet, "A ghost. I guess I had a little trouble with the scissors."

A moment later Snoopy pranced by all dressed up for Halloween.

"What is he supposed to be?" asked Lucy.

"A pilot from World War I," replied Charlie Brown.

"Now I've heard everything!" cried Lucy. "Okay, everyone, we'll go trick-or-treating and then head over to Violet's for the Halloween party. Everyone got their bag to fill?"

The trick-or-treaters passed Linus, who was settled in the pumpkin patch waiting for the Great Pumpkin.

"Have you come to sing pumpkin carols?" asked a hopeful Linus.

"Oh, good grief," cried Lucy, throwing her arms in the air.

Lucy turned to Sally. "Well, are you coming with us or not?"

Sally looked back and forth from Linus to her friends and then back at Linus.

After their friends left, Linus turned to Sally and said, "I'm glad you decided to stay."

"Do you really think he'll come?" asked Sally.

"Tonight the Great Pumpkin rises up and flies through the air bringing toys to children everywhere!" exclaimed Linus.

Meanwhile, the trick-or-treaters were starting their rounds in the neighborhood.

Each time someone opened their door, everyone cried, "Trick or treats!"

"Could I have an extra piece for my blockhead of a brother, please?" said Lucy, flashing a toothy grin. "He couldn't come with us because he's sitting in a pumpkin patch waiting for the Great Pumpkin."

Everyone met up on the sidewalk to size up what they received.

"It's so embarrassing that I have to ask for extra candy for that blockhead, Linus," said Lucy as she looked through her bag. "Looks like I got five pieces of candy."

"And I got a chocolate bar," added Violet.

"I got a gummy candy," said Peppermint Patty.

Charlie looked in his bag with disbelief, "I got a . . . rock!?"

The trick-or-treaters worked their way through the neighborhood. After every few houses, they stopped to take stock of what they had received.

"Nice!" exclaimed Lucy, "I got three cookies!"

"And I got a fudge bar," said Violet.

"Pack of gum," added Peppermint Patty.

"A rock!" cried Charlie Brown. "Not AGAIN!"

When everyone finished trick-or-treating, they started walking to Violet's house for the party. On their way, they passed by the pumpkin patch.

"Well, has the Great Pumpkin been by yet?" asked Violet with a smirk.

"You missed trick-or-treating, and now you are going to miss the Halloween party!" said Peppermint Patty.

Sally stepped forward and replied, "You all think you are *so* smart. You just wait. The Great Pumpkin is going to show. Linus knows what he is talking about."

With that, the kids left for Violet's house.

Once at the party, everyone started to partake in the Halloween festivities! Some were carving pumpkins, while others were getting ready to bob for apples.

"Out of my way," said Lucy, stepping up to the barrel. "Let me show you how it's done."

After a few seconds, Lucy pulled her head out of the bucket, but instead of just pulling out an apple...she pulled out a beagle!

"EWWWW!" cried Lucy. "My lips touched dog lips! *Gross!*"

Later at the pumpkin patch, Linus and Sally were still waiting for the Great Pumpkin to make an appearance.

Suddenly a rustling noise came from the middle of the pumpkin patch. They both turned toward the noise.

"Look!" Linus cried, pointing toward the moving shadow. "There he is! It's the Great Pumpkin. He's rising up from the pumpkin patch!"

Linus was so overwhelmed with excitement that . . . he fainted.

Within seconds, Linus came to and sat up. He looked around and asked, "What happened? Did I faint? Did he leave us any toys?"

"*I was robbed!*" Sally yelled. "Halloween is over, and I missed it! You kept me up all night waiting for the Great Pumpkin, and the only thing that came was a beagle!"

"When the Great Pumpkin comes, I'll still put a good word in for you," Linus yelled to Sally, but she was gone.

"Oh, Great Pumpkin," moaned Linus, "where *are* you?"

Later that night, Lucy woke up, looked at her clock, and went to check on her brother. He was not in his room. So she went outside and found him sleeping in the pumpkin patch. She picked him up, carried him home, and put him to bed.

The next morning, Charlie Brown and Linus met up.

"Well, another Halloween has come and gone, and all I got was a bagful of rocks," said Charlie Brown. "I guess the Great Pumpkin never showed?"

"You just wait until next time next year, Charlie Brown," cried Linus. "I'll sit in that pumpkin patch until the Great Pumpkin appears, and I'll be there!"